... readers ... Perfect for
be... ... author ... Bookshelf

"An endearing animal story"   *Mail on Sunday*

"A well-written, warmly sensitive and entertaining tale
with a lovely ending"   *Books for Keeps*

"Sparkling humour and wonderful characters are Dick
King-Smith's trademarks"   *Books for Your Children*

"Dick King-Smith has brought magic into the lives of
millions of children"   *Parents Magazine*

"Here is an author who has earned his stripes in the
world of animal writing, so you know you'll be in for a
good read"   *Belfast Telegraph*

Also available by Dick King-Smith, award-winning
author and creator of *Babe*:

Dick King-Smith

Horse Pie

Illustrated by Valerie Littlewood

YOUNG CORGI

HORSE PIE
A YOUNG CORGI BOOK 978 0 552 55432 9

First published in Great Britain by Doubleday,
an imprint of Random House Children's Publishers UK
A Random House Company

Doubleday edition published 1993
Young Corgi edition published 1994

This edition published 2006

12

The Random House Group Limited supports The Forest Stewardship
Council® (FSC®), the leading international forest-certification organisation.
Our books carrying the FSC label are printed on FSC®-certified paper.
FSC is the only forest-certification scheme supported by the leading
environmental organisations, including Greenpeace. Our
paper procurement policy can be found at
www.randomhouse.co.uk/environment

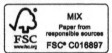

MIX
Paper from
responsible sources
FSC   FSC® C016897

Printed and bound in Great Britain by Clays Ltd, St Ives PLC

Set in 15/20pt Palatino by
Falcon Oast Graphic Art Ltd.

Addressess for companies within The Randon House Group Limited
can be found at: www.randomhouse.co.uk/offices.htm

Young Corgi Books are published by Random House Children's Publishers UK
61–63 Uxbridge Road, London W5 5SA,
a division of The Random House Group Ltd,

THE RANDOM HOUSE GROUP Limited Reg. No. 954009
www.randomhousechildrens.co.uk

A CIP catalogue record for this book is available from the British Library.

A Random House Group Company

CHAPTER ONE

"She'll have to go," said the donkeyman.

"Who?" said his son, Sam.

"Old Jenny. She's got so slow. Didn't you see that kid just now trying to make her walk a bit faster?

She was miles behind the others. She's past it."

Sam squiggled sand between his bare toes as he looked at the line of donkeys, waiting patiently for their next riders.

"What will happen to her, Dad?" he said.

"Have to see if they've got room for her at the Donkey Sanctuary," said his father.

"And if they haven't?"

"Cats' meat, I'm afraid," said the donkeyman.

"You mean . . . ?"

"Yes. Have to send the old girl to

the slaughterhouse."

"Oh, Dad, you couldn't! Not old Jenny!" Sam pleaded.

"Well, you think of a better idea then."

"Have a look at this," said the Manager of the Old Horses' Home to his stableman, a couple of days later.

"What is it, boss?"

"Letter from a kid. Son of the chap that keeps the beach donkeys at Easton-super-Mare."

The stableman read the letter.

"'. . . Donkey Sanctuary full up . . .

slaughterhouse . . . you are her last hope . . . Please, please!' Oh dear, pulls at your heart-strings, doesn't it, boss?"

The Manager nodded.

"He can't bear to think of her going to the knackers. We can make room for her, can't we?"

"Sure, boss," said the stableman. "What's one more among so many?"

*

5

And indeed there were a great many animals in the large, tree-shaded field in front of the Old Horses' Home. They were of all shapes and sizes, and all possible colours, and most of them were well past their prime. But amongst all the ancient ponies and horses were three giants who were, in fact, not old.

Captain and Ladybird were Shire horses, one black, one brown, and both with white stockings. Herbert was a Suffolk Punch – a chestnut like all his kind. All three were in good health but there was no work for them to do – tractors had taken their places.

Far larger and heavier and stronger than the rest, Captain and Ladybird and Herbert looked down their great Roman noses at all the other horses in the place.

One afternoon, the three giants stood side by side under a sycamore tree, watching as a horsebox came up the drive.

"Another old crock, I suppose," said Captain.

"A broken-down nag, I expect," said Ladybird.

"Or a cow-hocked pony," said Herbert.

They moved with ponderous

dignity towards the gate at the top corner of the field. Here the horsebox had stopped, and the stableman, who had come out to meet it, was opening the gate for it to reverse in.

Captain and Ladybird and Herbert watched as the tailgate was lowered. Then they shook their great heads in disgust as down it walked an old grey donkey.

"Good afternoon," she said. "My name is Jenny."

"It is not a good afternoon," said Captain.

"And as far as we are concerned,"

said Herbert, "your name is mud."

"You may not be aware," said Ladybird in the most patronizing of voices, "that this is a Home for horses."

"And not," said Captain, "for whatever sort of animal you may be."

"I think," said Herbert, blowing a snort of disgust through his large nostrils, "that it's an ass."

"Come away, boys," said Ladybird, "and leave the wretched creature. You don't know where it's been."

All three turned and walked

majestically back to the shade of the sycamore tree.

Chapter Two

Jenny stood watching the three big horses sadly. She thought of all her friends left behind on the beach, and she stretched out her neck and gave a series of creaking, groaning heehaws – the loudest,

most mournful noise imaginable.

Many of the other horses and ponies in the field looked up at this sound, and one animal detached itself from the herd and came over to the donkey. It was a little old skewbald pony, bony and swaybacked, and it walked right up to Jenny and touched noses with her and said in a croaky voice, "Welcome."

"I don't think I am," Jenny said. "Those big horses were horrid to me."

"Don't take no notice," said the skewbald pony. "They'm like that, them three. My name's Alfie, by the way."

"I'm Jenny."

"Toffee-nosed lot they are," said Alfie, nodding his head towards the sycamore tree and the three huge rumps, one black, one brown, one chestnut, of Captain and Ladybird and Herbert. "And they're big-headed with it, not to mention the size of their backsides."

"They are rather fat," said Jenny.

"Fat as butter," said Alfie. "Just the job for the rustlers."

"What are they?"

"Horse-thieves. Chaps that do

come round and nick horses."

"How do you know about these rustlers?" said Jenny.

"Heard tell about them from an old grey mare that used to live here. Dead now she is, but I can remember her telling me about these men that come round, at night usually, and steal livestock – cattle, sheep or horses. Once she saw a whole flock of sheep loaded up into a lorry and driven away."

"But why would they want to steal those three big horses?"

"To ship 'em across the water. To France – it's not far. Be worth their while to come for those three great lumps of lard. Why, they must weigh nearly a tonne apiece," said Alfie.

"But what would they send them to France for?" asked Jenny.

"For meat," said Alfie. "Didn't you know they eat horses in France?"

Jenny let out another ear-shattering bray.

"Eat *horses!*" she said. "How dreadful!"

"Oh, I don't know," Alfie said. "After all, your Englishman eats beef and lamb and pork. It's just that he wouldn't think of eating horses. He'd sooner keep 'em in a Home like this, costing hundreds of pounds to be looked after. But your Frenchman, he's got more sense. He sees a nice fat horse and he thinks to himself, '*Ooh là là!* Horse-pie!'"

"Do the French eat donkeys?" Jenny said.

"I don't reckon so," Alfie said.

"They wouldn't eat you, old girl, nor me, nor any of the old hat-racks round here. We'm all skin and bone. The rustlers wouldn't look at us, so don't worry your head about that."

But Jenny did worry. She was a

kindly animal by nature, and the thought of the possible danger to Captain and Ladybird and Herbert upset her very much. Rude and overbearing they might be, but the idea of those magnificent creatures being stolen and taken away by lorry and then by ship to France, there to be killed and made into horse-pie – that was horrifying!

CHAPTER THREE

For the rest of that day Jenny could think of nothing else as she grazed her way about the big field in Alfie's company.

Alfie, she noticed, though among the smallest of the ponies, was obviously a figure of some importance. He introduced her to the others as they met, and on the whole they greeted her in a friendly fashion. Though when a mare with a bit of breeding about her said, "An ass! What next?" she soon regretted it, for Alfie wheeled, quick as a cat, and his hind hooves beat a tattoo on her ribs.

But the three great carthorses were a different matter. One after another they worked their way close to the donkey and then, suddenly, lashed out or tried to bite her back. Once they lined up together and galloped

across the field towards her, snorting and whinnying, as though they meant to squash her into the very ground.

"Let's hope the rustlers get you!" shouted Alfie as they dodged out of the way. "Horse-pie, that's all you're good for!" But, of course, the thunder of hooves drowned his words.

"These rustlers," Jenny said. "When do they come?"

"At night," said Alfie. "Likely they'll have a big cattle-lorry parked down on the road, and then they'll come up the drive on foot, with halters."

"And how will they catch Captain and Ladybird and Herbert?"

"Sugar-lumps, I shouldn't wonder," said Alfie. "They'll go anywhere for a sugar-lump, they will. All the way to France, in fact."

"Alfie," said Jenny. "We must stop them."

"Stop who?"

"The rustlers."

"Whatever for, old girl? Good riddance to bad rubbish, I says. Nasty-tempered great things."

"I don't care about that," said Jenny. "They're still English horses and I'm an English donkey, and I'm not having them made into French horse-pies. We must stop the rustlers."

"Oh, nothing easier," said Alfie acidly. "You just waits by the gate and when the rustlers open it, you nips out and down the drive, and then you punctures all the tyres on the cattle-lorry."

"How do I do that?"

"Bite 'em."

For answer Jenny rolled back her lips, and Alfie could see that what few teeth she had left were blunt and brown and broken.

"Oh," he said. "Perhaps not."

"No," said Jenny, "but you've given me an idea."

"What?"

"'When the rustlers open the gate,' you said."

"Well?"

"There's only one gate to this field. There's no other way for Captain and Ladybird and Herbert to be taken out. The post-and-rail fence is too high, even if they could be made to jump it.

"So?"

"We wait until the rustlers are in the field with their halters and their sugar-lumps, and then we block the gate."

"You're joking, old girl," said Alfie. "You and me, stood in the gateway, trying to stop the rustlers leading those three monsters through? We'd get killed."

"We might," said Jenny, "but we needn't be alone. All the other horses and ponies could help. The

rustlers couldn't get through the whole herd."

The stableman, coming out to have a look round his horses, saw the skewbald pony and the donkey standing nose to nose. The pony was nodding his head vigorously.

"You've got something there, Jenny," Alfie said. "But they'd drive us out of the way after a bit. We shall need help from the stableman. How're we going to get him up in the middle of the night?"

"That's easy," Jenny said. "You leave that bit to me."

CHAPTER FOUR

"It's a funny thing, boss," said the stableman to the Manager of the Home, some days later, "but those horses are acting ever so strange. Every evening at dusk they gather round the gateway, in a tight mass, and then after a bit they move away, but not too far away. It's almost as if they were practising something."

"All of them?" the Manager said. "They all do this?"

"Not Captain or Ladybird or Herbert," the stableman said. "They don't seem to be part of it."

"Beneath their dignity perhaps," the Manager said.

"I watched particularly last night," the stableman said, "and it's old Alfie and that donkey that seem to be the ringleaders. They go around from horse to horse, and then the whole lot move over to the gateway. It's since that donkey came."

"Funny," said the Manager, "but you've reminded me of something. There's talk of rustlers in the district."

"Taking horses?"

"Yes. For the French trade. Put a stout chain and padlock on that gate, will you? It's the only one into the field."

That evening, Jenny and Alfie watched as the stableman carried out his orders.

"That's all right then," Jenny said.

"If the rustlers do come, they won't be able to get in."

"Be your age," said Alfie. "No, on second thoughts don't, you're old enough as it is. But they'll cut through that chain in a jiffy. They're professionals, these chaps, they know what to expect. Mark my words."

Alfie's words were marked a week later.

The evening parade of the herd around the gateway had just been dismissed, and only Alfie and Jenny still stood there in the dusk.

Suddenly Alfie put his muzzle against Jenny's long, hair-filled ear. "Look," he said softly.

They watched as a shadowy figure came walking up the drive. The man, they could see as he neared them, looked quite respectable – just an ordinary chap taking an evening stroll.

He stopped at the gate and leaned upon it, and looked about the darkening field. There was just enough light left to show, in their usual place beneath the sycamore, the three giant shapes.

"Watch," said Alfie as the man, after looking carefully around, put out a hand to examine the chain and padlock. Then he turned and went silently back.

"A rustler?" Jenny said.

"Looks like it. Haven't heard no lorry yet, it's too early."

"Shall we tell the others?" said Jenny. "We could always block the gateway to stop them getting in."

"No, no," said Alfie. "We wants them to come in and then we'll stop them getting out. Catch 'em red-handed. You go on down to the bottom by the road, old girl, and listen out for a lorry. Your ears are bigger than mine."

CHAPTER FIVE

Jenny was dozing by the rails when, around midnight, she heard a cattle-lorry approaching. It parked just outside the fence, on the grass verge of the road. Its lights were switched off and three men got out and very

quietly lowered the tailboard.

Jenny made off up the field.

"Look at that old moke!" one of the men said. "She's a walking skeleton."

"Don't think we'll bother with her," said a second man.

"Wait till you see the heavy horses," the third man said. "Why, they must weigh nearly a tonne apiece. Come on now, let's get a move on. I've got the bolt-cutters."

It was a darkish night, and the rustlers did not notice that, by the time they reached the gate, all the horses and ponies were alert, watching. The bolt-cutters made short work of the chain, and the men opened the gate, came into the field, closed the gate again, and set off towards the sycamore tree with their halters and their sugar-lumps. Behind them, the herd closed silently in front of the gateway.

Minutes passed, and then the horses saw the three rustlers making their

way back towards the gate. Behind each man walked a giant haltered shape, mumbling a sugar-lump.

"Right," said Alfie. "Stand firm, everybody." At his words, the ancients closed ranks even more tightly. Some faced the enemy, their yellow old teeth ready to bite. Some turned tail, prepared to kick the living daylights out of the rustlers. All stood waiting, dogged and determined.

"Get out of the way," the rustlers called, as quietly as they could. "Get out of it, you pack of miserable old deadbeats."

No-one moved.

Then Alfie's shrill neigh rang out.

"Captain! Ladybird! Herbert!" he cried. "Run for it! They're taking you to France, to make you into horse-pie!" At his words the three whirled away, dragging the halter-ropes from the men's hands, and

thundered off across the field.

"Now, Jenny!" called Alfie, and from inside the donkey's aged frame came those awful creaking, groaning heehaws, loud enough to wake the dead.

The stableman woke with a start. "Listen!" he said to his wife. "The old donkey's braying, in the middle of the night. That's not natural.

Something's wrong. Dial nine-nine-nine for the police. I'll get my gun," and he jumped out of bed.

Out in the field, the rustlers stood undecided, swearing, but Alfie had not done with them yet.

"Charge!" he cried, and now the whole herd of horses set off, straight at the rustlers, who threw themselves wildly over the fence and ran madly down the drive, pursued by the stableman. On the road a police car drew up beside the cattle-lorry.

CHAPTER FIVE

Down on the beach at Easton-super-Mare, the donkeyman leaned against one of his charges, reading the local newspaper. Suddenly he called to his son.

"Hey, Sam!" he cried. "Look at this!"

DONKEY FOILS RUSTLERS – DRAMA AT OLD HORSES' HOME

A warning from an old donkey led to the arrest of three horse-thieves who were attempting to steal stock from the Old Horses' Home. As luck would have it, the donkey chanced to bray loudly in the middle of the night and thus give the alarm. The police were able to intercept the rustlers, who will appear before local magistrates next week.

"That's got to be our old Jenny, Dad!" said Sam. "It must be. She's the only donkey in the place."

"Wonder how she knew they were rustlers," said the donkeyman. "What a funny thing."

*

"Funny thing," said the Manager of the Old Horses' Home to the stableman as they stood by the gate, a couple of days later. "The two Shires and the Suffolk Punch seem to have taken quite a fancy to that old donkey. They never went near her before except to rough her up."

"I know," said the stableman. "Look at them all now, boss, standing together under the sycamore tree, chummy as can be. It's almost as though they realized that they owe their lives to her. But of course they couldn't possibly know that."

Just then they heard a snickering beside them, and turned to see the old skewbald pony, baring his yellow teeth in what looked like a grin.

"Hello, Alfie," said the stableman. "What are you laughing at?"

THE END

ABOUT THE AUTHOR

Dick King-Smith was a Gloucestershire farmer until the age of 45, when he gave up farming to become a primary school teacher. Now a bestselling full-time author, his work has received many awards including a Bronze Medal for the Smarties Prize of 1997 for *All Because of Jackson* and the Children's Book Award in 1995 for *Harriet's Hare*.

In 1992, he was also voted Children's Author of the Year. In 1995, his top-selling title *The Sheep-Pig* was developed into a box-office movie, *BABE*, introducing hundreds of thousands of youngsters to his work. In 2005 he was the first recipient of the Peter Pan award.

